My Princess Collection

Cinderella

An Evening to Remember

Book Two

Adapted from *Princess Cinderella: An Enchanted Evening*,
written by Grace Windsor

For information address Disney Press, 114 Fifth Avenue,
New York, New York 10011-5690.
First Edition
Printed in China
3 5 7 9 10 8 6 4
ISBN 0-7868-4595-3

For more Disney Press fun,
visit www.disneybooks.com

Chapter One

Hello! I'm Princess Cinderella. I live in a palace with the Prince, and my life has become a dream come true.

When I was younger, I lived in the country with my father, a widower. I led a very happy life. Then one spring, Father married Lady Tremaine. I welcomed her and my stepsisters, Drizella and Anastasia, into our family. But they didn't like me—no matter how nice I was to them.

When Father passed away, my stepmother forced me to become a servant in my own house. I grew up scrubbing the floors, cooking meals, and waiting on my family. The chores were very tiring, and I dreamed of a better life. The animals of the house became my only friends. Two mice—Gus and Jaq—were my constant companions.

Chapter Two

One day, there was a knock at the door. It was a messenger from the palace. He handed me a letter from the King! It was an invitation to a ball. The King wished to introduce his son, the Prince, to the maidens in the kingdom. He had invited *everyone* to attend.

I couldn't wait to meet the Prince. And I had always dreamed about dressing up for a royal ball.

I rushed to show the invitation to my
stepmother. After she had read it aloud,
Anastasia and Drizella yelled, "You can't go!"

"It says *every* maiden," I reminded them.
They were always trying to leave me out, but
I was determined to go to the ball.

"I see no reason why you can't go," my stepmother said, "if you complete all your chores and find something suitable to wear."

I couldn't believe she was going to let me attend the ball. "Thank you so much!" I cried.

I was so excited that I practically skipped
to my room. I unpacked my only fancy
dress—an old one that had belonged to my
mother. It was pink and white and had a big
bow at the back. Gus and Jaq thought it
looked old-fashioned, but I knew all it needed
was a little work.

I couldn't wait to go to the palace. Maybe I would meet someone at the ball—and fall in love.

Suddenly, my stepsisters interrupted my thoughts. "Cinderella! Cinderella!" they shrieked.

The dress—and my dreams—would have to wait until later.

Chapter Three

I spent the entire day tending to my stepsisters. By the time I had finished, there was no time to work on my dress. I was very disappointed. But to my surprise, Jaq, Gus, and

the other mice had used my stepsisters' unwanted sashes and jewelry to transform my dress into a lovely gown. I even had a necklace of beads.

I thanked my friends and got ready just in time to catch up to my family.

When I showed them my dress, Drizella pointed to my neck and demanded, "Are those my beads?"

"And those are my sashes!" Anastasia cried, just as angrily.

All at once, my stepsisters began tearing at the dress, until it was completely in rags. My stepmother smiled and led my stepsisters out the door. I was all alone. My dreams were lost.

Chapter Four

I ran into the garden, buried my face in my hands, and began to cry. "There's nothing left to believe in," I said.

When I looked up, I saw a woman with a very kind face! She said she was my Fairy Godmother. "Come now," she said softly. "You can't go to the ball looking like that!"

With a wave of her wand, she transformed a pumpkin into a coach. And she changed the animals into attendants and magnificent horses.

Then she looked at my dress. Magic sparkled from her wand, turning my rags into a beautiful gown and my shoes into glass slippers. I felt like a princess!

She warned me that the magic would only last until the stroke of midnight. Then everything would return to normal.

I got into the coach, and the horses galloped quickly to the palace.

Once inside the ballroom, I saw a handsome stranger. He was bowing to Anastasia when our eyes met. I was so nervous, I didn't know what to say.

Then he asked me to dance. As we waltzed, my family watched us with jealousy in their eyes. It didn't matter, though. They didn't recognize me.

Afterward, we took a romantic walk in the garden. We were starting to fall hopelessly in love.

I was having such a wonderful time—

The time! It was almost midnight. There were only a few moments left before the magic would wear off. I raced outside without saying good-bye. In my haste, I left one of my glass slippers on the staircase.

At the final stroke of midnight, everything returned to normal. All I had left was one glass slipper and the memory of a truly enchanting evening.

Chapter Five

The next morning, as I combed my hair in my room, I hummed the song that had played the night before.

I was so happy. The King had ordered the Grand Duke and the royal footman to visit every house in the kingdom to search for the mysterious woman whose foot fit the glass slipper.

Suddenly, I jumped. My stepmother was watching me from the doorway. My heart sank as I realized she knew that *I* was the maiden who had danced with the Prince at the ball.

Downstairs, our footman announced the Grand Duke's arrival.

My stepmother left my room and locked the door behind her.

I could hear Anastasia downstairs, losing
her temper while trying to stuff her enormous
foot into my glass shoe. The Grand Duke was
starting to get impatient. I was afraid he
would leave, and . . . I just had to tell him
who I was—somehow.

Chapter Six

I had almost given up hope when I heard a sound at the door. Gus and Jaq had found the key! I ran downstairs to catch the Grand Duke.

As the footman approached me, my stepmother tripped him, causing the slipper to shatter on the floor! It was then that I revealed that I had the other slipper in my pocket. The Grand Duke slid it on my foot. It was a perfect fit!

Soon afterward, the Prince and I were married. The King welcomed me into the royal family as Princess Cinderella. What had begun as an enchanted evening had become a dream come true.